This book belongs to:

_____

MR BENN RED KNIGHT

MR BENN RED KNIGHT

DAVID McKEE

This edition first published in 2021 by Andersen Press Ltd.,
20 Vauxhall Bridge Road, London SW1V 2SA
First published by Dobson, London in 1967
Copyright © David McKee, 1967
The right of David McKee to be identified as the author and illustrator of this work
has been asserted by him in accordance with the Copyright, Designs and Patents Act, 1988.
All rights reserved. Printed and bound in China.
10 9 8 7 6 5 4 3 2 1
British Library Cataloguing in Publication Data available.
ISBN 978 1 83913 070 0

One morning Mr Benn received an invitation to a fancy dress party.
Really he wasn't very fond of parties, but he did like fancy dress and so he
decided to search the shops for something to wear. "After all," he thought,
"nothing exciting ever happens to me, I may as well make the most of it."

Mr Benn searched all day. He tried all the big stores, then the not so big stores, then the shops in the side streets, but all without luck. Nobody seemed interested in fancy dress, only in ordinary suits and things. Still Mr Benn kept trying and at last he was lucky. In a little narrow back lane he found a tiny old shop which was just packed with strange costumes.

In hurried Mr Benn quite excited at finding somewhere so wonderful. The shop bell tinkled and as if by magic there was suddenly a strange little man, with a moustache and an odd hat, standing in front of Mr Benn. "Good morning, sir, may I help you?" he asked.

Mr Benn was looking eagerly around the shop. "I wonder if I might borrow that suit of red armour in the window?" he replied. The little man seemed pleased. "Of course," he said. "Perhaps you would like to see if it fits." And he pointed to a door, marked FITTING ROOM in the corner of the shop.

Taking the armour and going through the door Mr Benn found himself in a small room just full of huge mirrors. He climbed into the armour and then laughed because the mirrors seemed to make the room full of red knights. Then he noticed the room had two doors, the one he came through marked SHOP and another marked TRYING ROOM.

"Well," said Mr Benn and without a thought opened the second door and walked through.

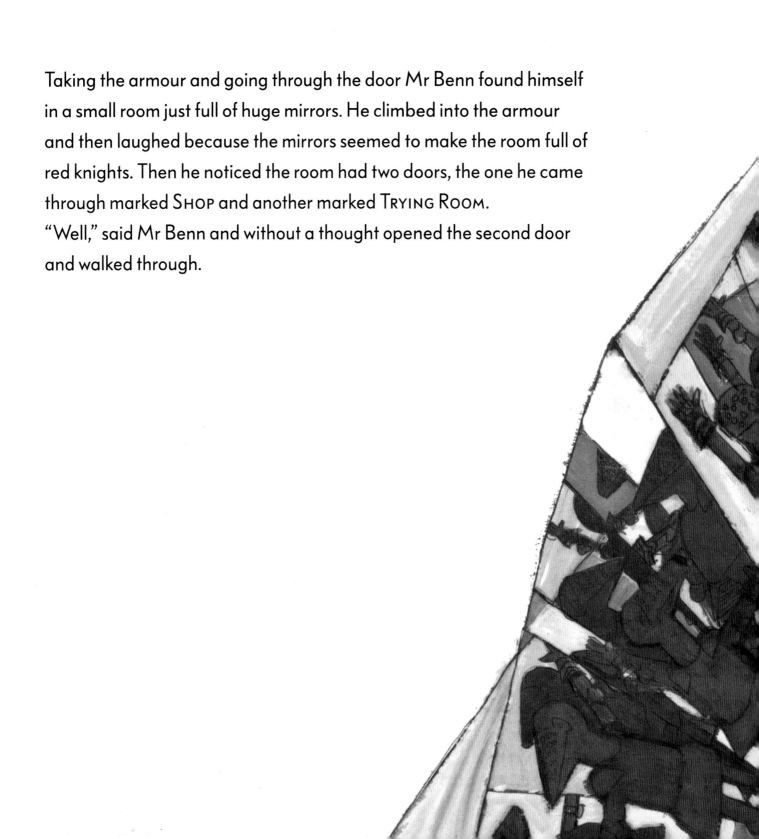

Instead of another room, Mr Benn was amazed to find himself surrounded by a desolate landscape. There was just barren, rocky countryside. Then he noticed that smoke was slowly rising from behind a large pile of rocks nearby. Mr Benn feeling bold in his suit of red armour decided to investigate.

Climbing up over the rocks he found that the smoke was coming from quite a large dragon. Of course Mr Benn guessed that it must be somebody else in fancy dress so he shouted down, "Hello, that's a wonderful outfit that you're wearing, and how on earth do you make that smoke?"

Flames burst from the dragon's mouth, "You can't fool me," he called back, "I know that you have been sent to kill me."

Slowly it dawned on Mr Benn that this was a real dragon and at the same time the dragon realised that this red knight didn't have a sword so he couldn't mean any harm.

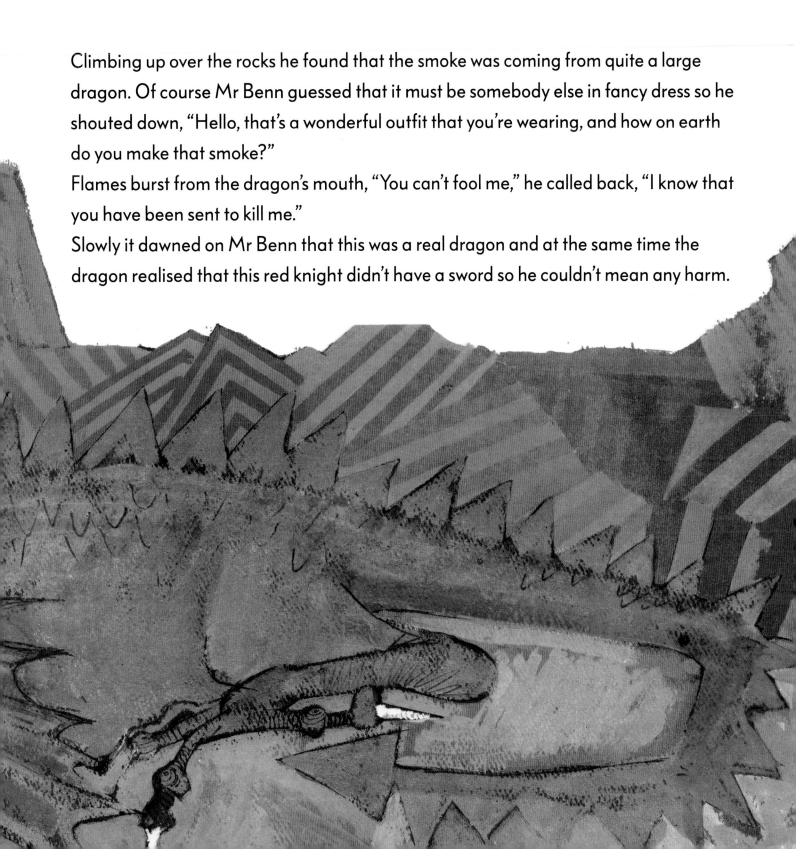

In a short time Mr Benn and the dragon were sitting down together with the dragon telling his story.

It seemed that the dragon had lived happily in a castle working hard at the family trade of firelighting for all the nearby houses. Everybody loved him especially the king. Then one day a visitor came to the castle with a new idea for lighting fires; he called it 'a match' and the visitor was a matchmaker.

Of course nobody wanted this new idea; after all the dragon was so reliable. The matchmaker wasn't content. He set fire to a barn or two and saw that the dragon got the blame. Gradually he made things so bad for the dragon that it was banished from the castle leaving the matchmaker to charge what he liked for the matches and so get rich. To make matters worse the king's favourite white horse had run away from the castle and the dragon was blamed for this as well. "Here he is you see," said the dragon showing Mr Benn the white horse standing on the other side of the rocks. "I have been looking after the horse but I'm much too afraid to return it."

"Come along my friend," said Mr Benn. "I'll help you. Show me where the castle is and I shall tell the king your story." This made the dragon very excited and they set off almost at once in the direction of the castle, the dragon leading the way and Mr Benn following on the white horse.

After a long journey the dragon stopped. "There is the castle," he said, and
sure enough the castle could be seen on a distant hill. "I'm afraid to go any
closer," continued the dragon. "I'll hide here among these trees and wait for
you to come back. Be careful and good luck!" With that they waved
goodbye and Mr Benn headed for the castle leaving the dragon in the trees.

By the time Mr Benn reached the castle the lookouts had already seen him and word had gone around that a brave red knight had slain the dragon and was returning the rescued horse.

Indeed Mr Benn had to say little for he was taken straight to the king to be rewarded.

When Mr Benn told the king the truth about the dragon the king was delighted. "That scoundrel of a matchmaker has been charging more and more for his matches," said the king. "He knows we have to have fires to cook and keep warm so he has been making a fortune while we are getting poorer and poorer."

The king called the guard and had the matchmaker thrown into the deepest, darkest dungeon. "He can wait there until I decide what to do with him," said the king.

As quickly as was possible the king had his guard ready to ride, then, leading the way with Mr Benn, they set off at a great pace to welcome the dragon back.

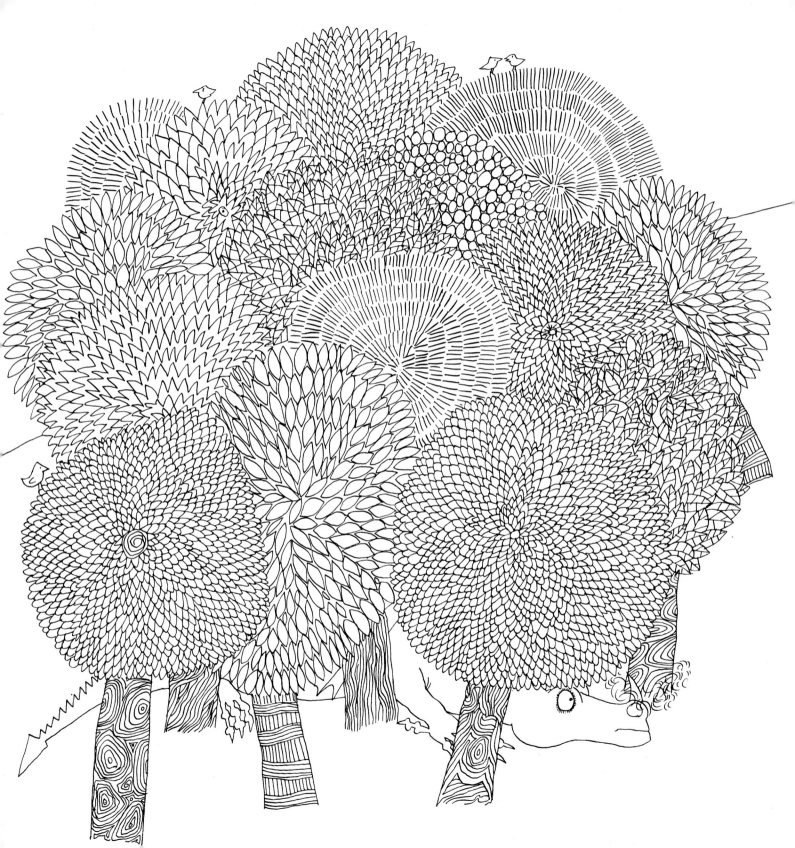

Mr Benn made them all stop some way from the trees where the dragon was hiding. Then he and the king left their horses and walked the rest of the way so as not to frighten the dragon.

The dragon was so happy that he would not let either Mr Benn or the king ride back on their horses, instead he insisted they both rode on his back. And so the triumphal procession entered the town and the castle, the guard led by the dragon carrying the king and Mr Benn.

Next the king made a speech to all his people. First he told them what had really happened to the dragon. Next he told them what was going to happen to the matchmaker. "I realise matches are more convenient for most of you than a dragon," he said, "and so I will let you have all the matches you want, free, and the matchmaker shall make them for nothing as his punishment. This will make things much easier for the dragon who will be my personal firelighter. After all," he smiled, "a king is entitled to something a little different." After the crowd had finished cheering the king said, "Tonight we will have a celebration feast with the Red Knight as guest of honour."

"Oh dear," Mr Benn said to himself, "after all that excitement I don't think I can face a party."

Soon after the speech was finished a little man with a moustache and an odd hat, who looked vaguely familiar to Mr Benn, asked him if he would like to change before the feast. He showed Mr Benn to a door.

"You will find fresh clothes inside, sir," he said. As soon as Mr Benn stepped through the door he recognised the fitting room of the

shop with all its mirrors. There were the other clothes sure enough
but they were Mr Benn's own clothes.

Stepping back into the shop he realised somehow he didn't want to go to the fancy dress party now. "I won't take it with me after all," said Mr Benn handing back the armour. "Right you are, sir," said the little man with the odd hat and he smiled as if he had expected to be told that. "But we shall be seeing you again, sir," he continued. "Oh, yes! I'll be back," answered Mr Benn and as he went out of the door he turned and added, "very soon."

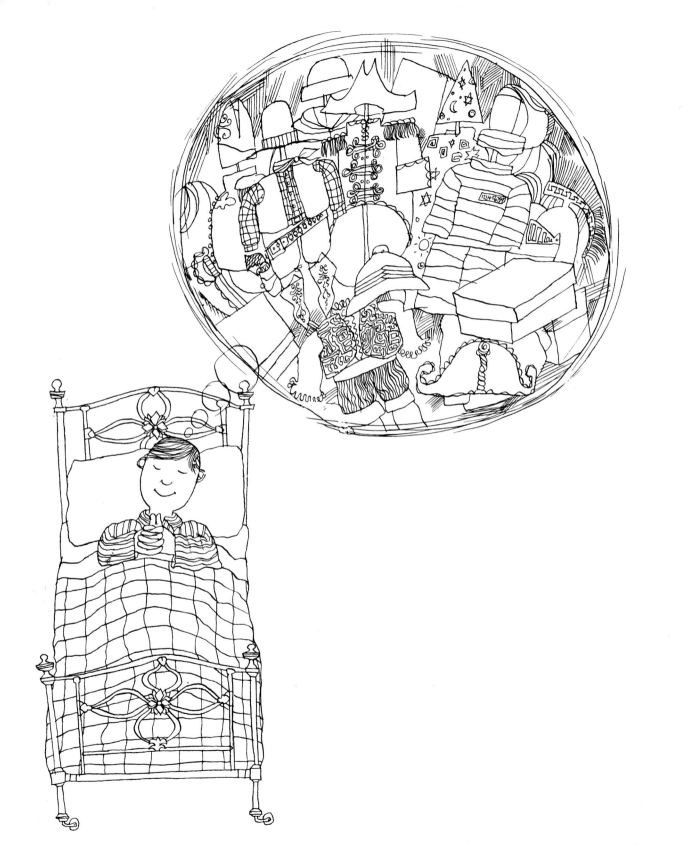

That night Mr Benn lay in bed and thought and thought. He thought of his adventure, and he thought of the shop, and he thought of the different costumes, the ones he had seen and the ones there might be. He tried to think which he would like to try on next time, but he fell asleep before he had time to decide.

Collect the original Mr Benn books!

MR BENN'S BIG GAME DAVID McKEE

MR BENN BIG TOP DAVID McKEE

MR BENN 123456789 DAVID McKEE